The Hole Truth

"And now," Penny said, "here's a coat that's a cut above the rest!"

Kendra strutted down the runway. Then Nancy noticed something strange.

"Bess? George?" Nancy asked slowly. "When I tried on the coat, did it have a big square hole in the back?"

"No way," George said. Then her eyes popped out. "Ohmygosh!"

Besh grabbed Nancy's arm. "Someone cut a hole in the black velvet coat!"

The Nancy Drew Notebooks

Available from MINSTREL Books

THE
NANCY DREW
NOTEBOOKS®

#32

The
Black Velvet Mystery

CAROLYN KEENE
ILLUSTRATED BY JAN NAIMO JONES

MINSTREL® BOOK

Published by POCKET BOOKS
New York   London   Toronto   Sydney   Tokyo   Singapore

A MINSTREL PAPERBACK *Original*

A Minstrel Book published by
POCKET BOOKS, a division of Simon & Schuster Inc.
1230 Avenue of the Americas, New York, NY 10020

ISBN: 0-671-03474-X

First Minstrel Books printing August 1999

10 9 8 7 6 5 4 3 2 1

Cover art by Joanie Schwarz

Printed in the U.S.A.

QBP/✗

1

Best-dressed Detective

I can't believe we're going to be in a real fashion show!" eight-year-old Nancy Drew said to her friends. They had just walked into Peppermint Penny's, their favorite store.

"I wonder if we'll get to keep the clothes we model," her best friend Bess Marvin said.

Nancy's other best friend, George Fayne, shook her head. "Bess! If you had any more clothes, your closet would burst."

Bess smiled at her cousin. "It already has!"

The girls were excited. The fashion show would be held right inside

Peppermint Penny's. The models were kids from River Heights. Two of those kids were Nancy and Bess.

"Wow!" Nancy said. "Peppermint Penny's has never looked like this."

The girls looked around the store. A long red carpet ran from the back of the store to the front. Rows of chairs lined both sides of the carpet. Tied to each chair was a colorful balloon.

Above the racks of clothes were signs that read, Back to School.

"I don't get it," George said. "We have three weeks of summer vacation left. Why do all the signs say, Back to School?"

Nancy smiled. "So we can have a back-to-school fashion show!"

"Nancy, look!" Bess said. She pointed to a clock on the wall. "It's already one o'clock. The fashion show starts in just an hour."

Nancy saw the owner of the store, Penny, rush by. She and her salesgirl, Tara, were counting chairs.

Penny had short dark hair and blue eyes. She was wearing black pants and a shiny red blouse. Tara had brown hair and freckles. She wore a striped T-shirt and tan pants.

"I'll bet Penny and Tara are as excited as we are," Nancy said.

"And probably as nervous," Bess said. She turned to George. "Did you change your mind about being in the show?"

"Not unless I can model my jeans and soccer shirt," George said.

Bess rolled her eyes, but Nancy giggled. As cousins, Bess and George were nothing alike.

"That's okay, George," Nancy said. "You're going to help us change into our outfits during the fashion show."

The other kids who were going to be models began to arrive. Nancy saw eight-year-old Kendra Cartwright and nine-year-old Scott Mancuso. Then Nancy saw someone she didn't expect.

"Don't tell me Brenda Carlton is in the fashion show," Nancy said, groaning.

"Maybe she's modeling *snooty pants*," Bess said giggling.

"I heard that, Bess Marvin!" Brenda snapped. She walked over to the girls.

"Since when do *detectives* model clothes?" Brenda asked Nancy.

"Since today," Nancy said.

Nancy was the best detective at Carl Sandburg Elementary School. But she also liked nice clothes.

"What about *you*, Brenda?" Nancy asked. "What are you doing here?"

Brenda's eyes lit up. "I'm writing an article for the *Carlton News*," she said.

"What else is new?" George muttered.

The *Carlton News* was Brenda's own newspaper. She wrote it at home on her computer.

"Are you writing about the new clothes in the fashion show?" Bess asked.

"No," Brenda said. She gave a sly smile. "I'm writing a gossip column."

Nancy stared at Brenda. Gossip was another word for rumors.

"Gossip can be mean, Brenda," Nancy said. "Especially when it's not true."

Brenda flipped her dark hair over her shoulder. "Who says it won't be true?"

"You *have* made up stories before, Brenda," George said.

Brenda looked angry. "I won't have to make these up. There'll be plenty of juicy things to write about here!"

Nancy watched as Brenda left to look at a stack of sweaters.

"What can be worse than having Brenda Carlton here today?" Bess asked.

George pointed to the door. "How about Orson Wong?"

Nancy saw eight-year-old Orson walking into the store with his brothers, the six-year-old twins, Lonny and Lenny. The twins were going to model boys' clothes.

"We're going to be in a fashion show!" Lonny shouted as they ran over.

"We're handsome!" Lenny bragged.

"Not with ice cream all over your face," George said.

The twins grinned as they crunched on their favorite chocolate Panda Bars.

Then Nancy noticed that Orson was wearing a black beret on his head.

"Is that part of your magician's costume, Orson?" Nancy asked. She knew that Orson wanted to be a magician when he grew up.

"I'm not a magician anymore," Orson declared. He reached into his pocket and pulled out a folded piece of paper. "Orson the Awesome is now Orson the *Artist!*"

He held up the paper. It was covered with one big splotch of white paint.

"What did you do?" George asked, "Spill your milk?"

"You know nothing about great art!" Orson snapped. He pointed to the painting. "This is a picture of a polar bear. A polar bear in a snowstorm."

Nancy tilted her head. She couldn't see a polar bear *or* a snowstorm.

"Tell them what you're going to paint next, Orson," Lenny said.

"For my next project," Orson announced, "I'm going to paint insects."

"Bugs?" Bess gasped.

Orson nodded. "But this time I'm going to paint them on black velvet. Like those paintings you see in fancy diners."

"Where are you going to get all those bugs?" George asked.

"I already have the bugs," Orson said. "But I can't find the black velvet."

Just then Penny called for attention. "Will everyone working on the fashion show please follow me into the stockroom?"

"That's us!" Nancy said excitedly.

Orson stayed behind while the other kids followed Penny to the room in back of the store. It was filled with piles of boxes and racks of clothes.

Nancy and Bess knew which clothes they would be modeling. The kids had tried on the clothes a few days ago. After Penny chose what they would wear, she hung nametags over each outfit.

"There's my pretty skirt set," Nancy said. She could see her nametag hanging over the pink plastic hanger.

Penny raised her hands for attention. "During the fashion show you can all change behind the boxes," she said. "Girls on the right side of the room, and boys on the left."

Lenny turned to Nancy, Bess, and George. "And you'd better not peek!"

Lonny waved his Panda Bar. "Or else!"

"Lonny. Lenny," Penny said. "You're not allowed to eat around the clothes."

"But if we put the Panda Bars in our pockets, they'll melt," Lenny whined.

"There's a mini fridge against that wall," Penny said, pointing. "You can put them in there until after the show."

The twins grumbled as they walked toward the fridge.

"Now," Penny said. "Are there any questions about the fashion show?"

Nancy raised her hand. "Why are we modeling winter clothes in August?"

"That's a good question, Nancy," Penny said. "Stores always show clothes one season early, so people can look forward to buying new clothes."

"You mean you sell bathing suits in February?" Bess gasped. "Brrr!"

Nancy saw Tara rush into the stockroom. She was holding a big flat box. "This has just arrived, Penny," she said. "It's from Lulu's of Paris."

"It's the coat!" Penny said excitedly. She ripped the box open and smiled. "I didn't expect it so soon."

Penny carefully pulled a girl's coat from the box. It was made of black velvet and had shiny silver buttons.

"It's beautiful!" Nancy gasped.

"Excuse me!" a voice called.

Nancy and the others whirled around. A woman with silver hair and gold dangly earrings was standing at the door. There was a soft, flowered handbag on her shoulder.

"Are you Peppermint Patty?" she asked.

"I'm Penny," Penny said.

"I am Mrs. Vanderpool," the woman said. "And I would like to buy some hair barrettes for my babies."

"How old are your little girls?" Penny asked.

Mrs. Vanderpool pulled two tiny Yorkshire terrier dogs from her bag. "They're only three years old," she said.

"Doggies!" Lenny cried.

"Let's pet them!" Lonny said.

Mrs. Vanderpool placed her dogs down. She looked at the coat. Then she touched it. "That is the most stunning black velvet I have ever seen. I *must* have it."

"But it would never fit you, Mrs. Vanderpool," Penny said.

"Not for *me!*" Mrs. Vanderpool declared. "My dogs need new collars for their coats. That black velvet is the perfect material."

"Your dogs wear coats in August?" Scott Mancuso asked.

Mrs. Vanderpool nodded. "Air-conditioning makes them shiver."

Penny shook her head. "Sorry. But we need the coat for the fashion show."

"Phooey!" Mrs. Vanderpool snapped. She picked up her dogs and marched out.

"Mrs. Vanderpool lives in one of the biggest houses in River Heights," Nancy told Bess and George. "My dad showed it to me while we were taking a walk one day."

"If her house is so big, why does she have such small dogs?" George asked.

Penny held the coat up again.

"Now," Penny said. She looked around the room. "Who's going to model this?"

All of the girls raised their hands. Penny smiled at Nancy.

"Me?" Nancy gasped.

"You," Penny said. She helped Nancy put on the coat.

"It looks so nice with your reddish blond hair, Nancy," Bess said.

Nancy felt like a princess. Until Kendra Cartwright shouted out, "It's not fair! That coat should go to me!"

2

Wear and Tear!

What?" Nancy gasped.

She stared at Kendra, who was tall and always wore very fashionable clothes to school.

"Why should you wear the coat, Kendra?" Penny asked.

"Because I went to the Picture Perfect Modeling School this summer," Kendra said. She put her hand on her hip and twirled around. "See?"

Penny walked over to Nancy. She tugged at the coat's sleeves.

"Uh-oh," Penny said. "These sleeves are a bit long on you, Nancy."

Nancy stretched her fingers. "They don't feel long," she said.

"This coat really does belong on someone a bit taller," Penny said.

"Like me!" Kendra cried happily.

"I'm sorry, Nancy," Penny said.

Nancy was sorry, too. She loved the black velvet coat and wanted to wear it in the fashion show.

"It's okay, Penny." Nancy sighed. She took off the coat.

As she handed it to Kendra she saw Orson peeking into the back room. He had a very sneaky look on his face.

Orson is always up to something, Nancy thought. What's he up to now?

Kendra tried on the coat. She smiled and twirled around and around.

"Isn't she dizzy yet?" George whispered.

"Let's go out on the floor," Penny said. "I want to show you where you'll be modeling your clothes."

Nancy, Bess, and George began to follow Penny. Then Brenda jumped out in front of them with a pad and pencil.

"I was hiding behind a clothes rack," Brenda said. "I got the whole scoop."

"What scoop?" Nancy asked.

"You wanted that coat didn't you, Nancy?" Brenda demanded.

Nancy shrugged. "Sure, but—"

"And you're mad because Kendra got the coat. You're jealous because she's so pretty. And most of all, you want to get even!"

There Brenda goes again, Nancy thought, making up nasty stories.

"The coat didn't fit," Nancy said.

"Let's go, Nancy," Bess said. "She just wants a gossipy story for her paper."

The girls left the stockroom. Nancy saw lots of people walking into the store.

They must be here for the fashion show, Nancy thought with a smile.

She looked around the store. Mrs. Vanderpool was spinning a rack of hair barrettes. Orson was standing in front of a mirror and making faces.

"This carpet will be your runway,"

Penny said. She pointed to the long red carpet right outside the stockroom.

Kendra raised her hand. "At the modeling school we called it a catwalk."

"Meow! Meow!" Lenny howled.

Penny laughed. "Why don't we practice walking up and down the runway? Lonny and Lenny, you go first."

The twins looked at each other.

"Okay," Lenny said. "Ready, set, go!"

Everyone stared as the twins raced up and down the carpet.

"What are you doing?" Penny asked.

"It's a runway," Lonny said.

"So we're running!" Lenny said.

"It's just called a runway," Penny corrected. "You should walk nice and slow so everyone can see your clothes."

After all the kids got to practice, Penny looked at the clock. "It's almost two o'clock," she said. "It's time to change into your first outfits."

The kids rushed back into the stockroom. They ran behind the boxes and began to change. Nancy saw shoes,

scarves, and sweaters flying everywhere.

"Where are my blue tights?"

"I can't find my vest!"

Nancy pulled on a plaid skirt and a
dark green turtleneck. Bess struggled to
tie the bow on her blue party dress.

"George!" Bess called. "I need help!"

"I've never worn a dress like that,"
George complained.

"Nancy, you'll be first," Penny called.
"Are you ready?"

Nancy's heart jumped. "I'm ready!"

Tara turned on a CD player as Nancy
walked out of the stockroom.

Nancy stepped onto the red carpet
and glanced around. The chairs were
filled with people, and Nancy's stomach
was filled with butterflies.

"Here's Nancy modeling a crisp back-
to-school skirt and sweater," Penny
announced to the audience.

Nancy walked slowly and carefully
down the red carpet. When she reached
the end she smiled and twirled around.

"Thank you, Nancy," Penny said.

Nancy was about to walk into the stockroom when the Wong twins crashed into her.

"Out of our way!" Lenny ordered.

The boys ran past Nancy with balloons in their hands.

"And here are Lonny and Lenny showing us that twins don't *always* dress alike," Penny said.

The rest of the fashion show was exciting. Nancy and Bess modeled three more outfits. Then it was time for the black velvet coat.

"I hope everyone has noticed me," Kendra said. She quickly slipped on the coat. Then she strutted out of the room.

"Let's watch," Nancy told Bess and George. They peeked out of the stockroom.

"And now," Penny said. "Here's a coat that's a cut above the rest!"

Kendra strutted down the runway. Then Nancy noticed something strange.

"Bess? George?" Nancy asked slowly.

"When I tried on the coat, did it have a big square hole in the back?"

"No way," George said. Then her eyes popped out. "Ohmygosh!"

Bess grabbed Nancy's arm. "Someone cut a hole in the black velvet coat!"

"The coat has a black lining underneath," Nancy whispered. "Maybe no one else will notice."

But just then a little boy jumped up from his seat.

"Look, Mommy!" he shouted. "There's a big hole in the back of that coat!"

3
Clues ... Bad News!

"Oh, no!" Nancy gasped.

The store was silent. Kendra looked over her shoulder at the back of the coat.

"It looks like Swiss cheese," a girl in the audience snickered.

Kendra covered her face with her hands. She ran back up the carpet toward the stockroom.

"The show is over, ladies and gentlemen," Penny said quickly. "Thank you all for coming."

Kendra almost knocked Nancy over as she burst through the stockroom door.

"They were laughing at me!" Kendra cried as she yanked off the coat. "I want to be a supermodel—not a clown!"

"Well, at least they noticed you," Scott said cheerfully.

Kendra stared at Scott. Then she sobbed and ran out of the room.

"What did I say?" Scott asked.

Penny marched into the back room. She went straight to Kendra's rack.

"What are these doing on the floor?" Penny asked. She picked up a pair of sewing scissors. "They're usually in my sewing basket."

I'll bet those were the scissors that cut the coat, Nancy thought.

"Will the person who ruined the coat be honest and come forward?" Penny asked.

When no one came forward, Penny sighed. "I'll be in the store all day if any of you has something to tell," she said. Then she left the room.

"Ye-es!" Brenda cheered. "I knew that something juicy would happen today!"

"How can you be so mean, Brenda?" Bess asked. "The fashion show was ruined!"

"I know," Brenda said. She waved her pad. "But I have all the gossip I need."

Nancy and her friends stared as Brenda strutted out of the room.

"She makes me barf," George said.

"Forget about Miss Snooty Pants," Nancy said. "We have more important things to do."

"Like what?" Bess asked.

"Like finding out who ruined the black velvet coat," Nancy said.

Bess's blue eyes shined. "You mean you're going to solve another mystery, Nancy?" she asked.

"But you didn't bring your detective notebook to the fashion show," George said.

Nancy smiled. Her blue detective notebook was where she wrote down all her clues and suspects. She almost never left home without it.

"Oh, yes, I did," Nancy said. She walked over to her own clothes and pulled her notebook from the pocket of her shorts.

"It's the perfect accessory for all fashionable detectives," Nancy added.

"And blue *is* your color," Bess joked.

George looked at her watch. "We have some time before my dad picks us up."

"Great," Nancy said. "Let's change into our own clothes and look for clues."

The other models went home, but Nancy, Bess, and George stayed in the stockroom.

After Nancy and Bess changed, they sat on a crate.

Bess and George looked over Nancy's shoulder as she wrote, "The Case of the Cut-up Coat" on a fresh page. Then under the word "Clues," she wrote "Scissors."

"I don't get it, Nancy," Bess said. "How could anyone cut up the coat when this room was full of people?"

"And I was back here all through the fashion show," George said.

"This is what I think," Nancy said. "The stockroom was empty when

24

Penny showed us the runway. And we were practicing for a good fifteen minutes."

"So the person who cut the coat could have sneaked in then," George said.

Nancy nodded. "The scissors are a great clue. Let's look for some more."

The girls searched the back room. Suddenly Bess let out a huge shriek.

"I found it! I found it!" Bess cried.

"Another clue?" Nancy asked.

"No!" Bess said. She held up a dark purple beret. "I found the *perfect* hat for my new fall jacket! Isn't it pretty?"

"Give me a break," George groaned.

"Bess," Nancy said, "we're looking for new *clues*, not new clothes."

Bess sighed and put down the hat.

As Nancy looked under the rack where the black coat was hanging, something shiny caught her eye.

"Bess! George!" Nancy called. "I think I found something."

Nancy picked up the shiny object. It was gold with big pearls attached.

"It's a clip-on earring," Bess said.

Nancy rolled the earring in her hand. "These look like the same earrings Mrs. Vanderpool was wearing," she said.

"Why would she have been near the coat rack?" Bess asked.

George snapped her fingers. "She wanted that coat for her little dogs."

Nancy slipped the clue in her pocket. "We have our first suspect," she said. "It's Mrs. Vanderpool."

"Who else would have wanted to cut up the coat?" George asked.

"Someone *mean*," Bess said.

The girls looked at each other.

"Brenda!" they exclaimed together.

"Brenda wanted a gossipy story for her paper," Nancy said. "She might have cut the coat so she could write about it."

Nancy wrote Brenda's name under her list of suspects. Then, below Brenda's name, she wrote, "Orson Wong."

"Orson?" Bess said. "Why would he want to cut up the coat?"

"He said he needed black velvet for those gross paintings of his," Nancy said. "And I did see him looking at the coat."

Bess shook her head. "Sneaky, sneaky, sneaky!"

"Three suspects and two clues is a great start," Nancy said. She shut her notebook. "Let's meet tomorrow to work on the case."

That evening, Nancy helped Hannah make a salad for dinner. Hannah Gruen had been the Drews' housekeeper since Nancy was only three years old.

"So how does it feel to be a famous model?" Hannah asked as she washed a green pepper.

Nancy looked up from the lettuce she was tearing. "Modeling clothes was fun, Hannah," Nancy said. "But I'd still rather be a detective."

"You mean you prefer clues to shoes?" Hannah joked.

Nancy giggled. She was about to tell

Hannah about the case when the door-bell rang.

"Oh, dear," Hannah said. "My hands are all wet."

"I'll see who it is," Nancy said.

Nancy ran to the front door. She stood on her toes and looked out the peep hole. No one was there.

"Who is it?" Nancy called.

When no one answered, Nancy opened the door very slowly. She saw a piece of paper on the doorstep.

What's this? Nancy wondered.

Nancy picked it up and groaned. It was the *Carlton News*. On the top of the page were the words "Gossip! Gossip! Gossip!"

Brenda sure works fast, Nancy thought. But when she started to read, her stomach did a triple flip.

"'Who with reddish blond hair would cut up a gorgeous black velvet coat?'" Nancy read out loud. "'Word has it that she was mad! Word has it that she was jealous! And it's no *mystery* that she was catty on the catwalk. *Mew! (Rhymes with?)'*"

Nancy looked up from the paper and gasped. "Oh, no! *Mew* rhymes with *Drew!*"

4

Follow That Ponytail!

Brenda is accusing me of cutting up the coat!" Nancy complained to Bess and George the next morning.

The girls had gotten permission to walk to Peppermint Penny's to look for more clues.

"Why would Brenda accuse you?" George asked.

"She said I was mad because Kendra got to wear the coat instead of me," Nancy said.

"Well, at least Brenda didn't mention your name," Bess said.

"She didn't have to, Bess," Nancy insisted. "She gave more hints than in a game of charades."

"Don't worry, Nancy," George said. "How many kids in River Heights read that stupid paper anyway?"

Just then two nine-year-old girls from Carl Sandburg Elementary School walked by. They looked at Nancy and giggled.

"Mew! Mew! Drew! Drew!" one of the girls said. Then they both walked away.

"Great." Nancy sighed.

The three friends walked up Main Street. Suddenly Bess grabbed Nancy's arm.

"Speaking of Miss Snooty Pants," Bess whispered. "Look who's coming out of Peppermint Penny's!"

Nancy glanced across the street. Brenda and her mother were walking out of the store. Mrs. Carlton was carrying a big shopping bag. Brenda's ponytail bounced as she followed her mother.

"I wonder which outfit Brenda bought," Bess said.

"Probably a witch's hat and a broom," George muttered.

Nancy watched Mrs. Carlton walk into a nearby food shop. Brenda stayed outside to look in the store window. But when she turned around, Nancy jumped.

"Bess! George!" Nancy said in a low voice. "Brenda is wearing a black bow on her ponytail. It looks like it's velvet!"

"You think it's the same black velvet as the coat?" George asked.

"If it is," Nancy said, "then we'll know that Brenda was the cut-up."

"Isn't all velvet the same?" Bess asked.

"The velvet on the coat was thick and soft," Nancy said. "I'll never forget it."

George stared across the street. Her eyes were narrow.

"If I could just yank the bow off Brenda's ponytail," she said. "Then we could check it out."

"She'd have to be standing very still," Bess said. "And Brenda Carlton never stands still."

Just then Nancy saw something in

Peppermint Penny's window. It was a wooden statue that wore clothes and looked like a real girl. Nancy knew the statue was called a dummy—and it gave her an idea.

"I know a way to get Brenda to stand perfectly still," Nancy said slowly.

"How?" Bess asked.

Nancy turned to Bess. "Bess, how would you like to be a dummy?"

"That's mean!" Bess cried.

"I mean a *mannequin*," Nancy said. "That's a fancy word for the dummies in the store windows."

"You mean I have to stand perfectly still?" Bess asked. "Like a statue?"

"I'll do it, too," Nancy said. "If Brenda plays along, George can sneak up behind her and pull off her bow."

"Can you do it, George?" Bess asked. "Can you sneak up behind Brenda?"

"No problem," George said. She pointed to her feet. "What do you think sneakers are for?"

George waited across the street while

Nancy and Bess hurried over to Brenda.

"Hi, Brenda," Nancy called.

Brenda's black bow flapped as she turned around. "Have you seen my new gossip column?" she asked slyly.

"Yes," Nancy said. "But we have no idea who you're writing about."

"Not a clue," Bess said.

Nancy counted to three. Then she froze like a statue. Bess did the same.

"What are you doing?" Brenda asked.

"Can't you tell?" Bess asked with her hands on her head. "We're dummies."

"That's for sure!" Brenda sneered.

"We're *mannequins*," Nancy corrected. She posed with one hand on her hip.

"Why?" Brenda asked.

"Penny asked us to model clothes in her window," Nancy said. "So we're practicing to stand perfectly still."

Brenda began to walk away. "That's the weirdest thing I ever heard."

"That's okay, Brenda," Nancy said quickly. "Not everyone can do it."

"Not even you," Bess said.

Brenda froze. She turned around. "What do you mean?" she snapped. "I can stand still if I want to!"

Brenda jutted her arms in the air. She stuck up her chin. "See?"

Perfect! Nancy thought. Brenda even has her back to George.

"Now hold that pose for as long as you can," Nancy said.

From the corner of her eye, Nancy saw George crossing the street. She was tiptoeing slowly toward Brenda.

All systems go, Nancy thought.

Suddenly Nancy heard a loud buzz. A big fly was circling around her head!

Bzzz! Bzzz! Bzzz!

Nancy wanted to wave it away but she couldn't. She had to stand still.

Nancy crossed her eyes as the fly landed on the tip of her nose.

Hurry up, George, Nancy thought. She wiggled her nose. Hurry up!

But it was too late. Her nose itched and she began to sneeze. "Ahh-ahhh-chooo!"

The girls broke their poses.

Brenda whirled around. "George Fayne!" she cried. "What were you doing behind my back?"

George shrugged as she held the black bow in her hand.

"My bow!" Brenda cried. She reached back and touched her ponytail. "You were stealing my black velvet bow!"

5

Snip, Snip—Hooray!

George wasn't stealing your bow," Nancy insisted.

"Yes she was!" Brenda said. "And you made her do it!"

"Me?" Nancy asked.

Brenda nodded. "You're not just a cut-up, Nancy. You're a thief!"

Nancy grabbed the bow from George's hand. "If I'm the cut-up, how do you explain this?"

As Nancy waved the bow in front of Brenda, she noticed a piece of paper stapled to the back. It was a price tag from Peppermint Penny's.

"My mother just bought me that

bow," Brenda said. "I wanted to wear it out of the store. Now, give it back!"

Nancy felt the bow in her fingers. It didn't feel as thick and soft as the coat.

"Sorry, Brenda," Nancy said. She held out the bow. "We were just trying to find the real cut-up."

Brenda snatched the bow. "I know who the real cut-up is. And I've only begun to write about her!"

The girls looked at each other.

"In fact," Brenda said, sticking out her chin. "I'm making the *Carlton News* a daily paper. So I can write my gossip column every day."

"Yippee," George muttered.

Brenda tied the bow around her ponytail. Then she ran to her mother.

"Come on," Nancy said. "Let's go into Peppermint Penny's. Maybe Penny can help us."

But when the girls went inside the store, Penny would not let them look for clues.

"Just a peek?" George asked Penny.

Penny shook her head. "I'm keeping the stockroom locked from now on."

"I understand," Nancy said. But as they walked toward the front of the store, Nancy noticed something on top of the jewelry counter. It was a copy of the *Carlton News*.

"Oh, no," Nancy whispered. "Now Penny probably suspects me, too!"

"Thanks to the *Carlton News*," George said angrily.

The girls left Peppermint Penny's. They sat on a bench next to the store. Nancy took out her blue notebook and scratched out Brenda's name.

"We still have two suspects," Nancy said. "Mrs. Vanderpool and Orson Wong."

"Orson lives right near your house, Nancy," George said. "Why don't we check him out after lunch?"

"Nancy always walks her dog, Chocolate Chip, after lunch, George," Bess said. "Right, Nancy?"

Nancy nodded. But then she had an idea.

"Bess, George," she said. "Lonny and Lenny Wong love dogs, right?" she asked.

"They sure do," George said.

"Maybe while the twins pet Chip, they'll tell us everything we need to know about Orson," Nancy said.

"Good thinking, Nancy!" George said.

When the three friends got back to Nancy's house, Bess and George called for permission to stay and eat lunch.

After munching on Hannah's tuna salad sandwiches, Nancy, Bess, and George walked Chocolate Chip to Orson Wong's block.

"I hope we don't have to search Orson's room," Bess said.

"You mean because of his pet iguana?" Nancy asked.

"No," Bess said. She grabbed her nose. "Because of his smelly socks."

Mrs. Wong was working in her garden when the girls approached the house. She smiled as she petted Chip.

"Hi, girls!" Mrs. Wong said.

"Hello, Mrs. Wong," Nancy said. "Are Orson, Lonny, and Lenny home?"

"They sure are," Mrs. Wong said. "The twins are upstairs finger painting. And Orson is in the backyard. He's painting, too."

"Is Orson painting bugs?" Bess asked, wrinkling her nose.

"Yes," Mrs. Wong said. "On some kind of black material."

Nancy froze. Black material?

"Mrs. Wong," Nancy said. "Could we go in the back and say hi to Orson?"

Mrs. Wong nodded. "I'm sure he'd love a visit from his friends."

Nancy could hear George gag at the word "friends."

"Thank you, Mrs. Wong," Nancy said. She tugged at Chip's leash.

Nancy, Bess, and George ran around the house to the back yard.

"There he is!" Nancy whispered.

Orson was sitting at an easel. On a small table next to him was a glass jar.

43

"You're in my light," Orson complained as the girls walked closer. "And your dog is giving Wally the willies."

"Wally?" Nancy asked.

Orson pointed to the glass jar. Inside the jar was a big brown bug with long legs.

"Ugh—gross!" Bess gagged.

"People call Wally a water bug," Orson explained. "But I like to think of him as a great big cockroach!"

Nancy looked over Orson's shoulder. Sure enough, he was painting the bug on a small piece of black material.

Nancy glanced down and saw something else. On the ground next to Orson was a small pile of the same material.

"Is that black *velvet* you're painting on, Orson?" Nancy asked.

Orson held up his paintbrush. "Maybe it is, maybe it isn't."

Nancy reached for the material. "Where did you get it?"

Orson grabbed the material and sat on it. "None of your beeswax!" he snarled.

George marched up to Orson. "A black velvet coat was cut up at Peppermint Penny's yesterday."

"Did you do it, Orson?" Nancy asked.

Orson shrugged. "Maybe I did, maybe I didn't."

Chocolate Chip ran over to Orson. She tugged at the material under him.

"Hey, cut it out!" Orson cried.

Nancy was about to help her dog when she heard giggling. It sounded like Lonny and Lenny.

A sly smile spread across Orson's face.

"Oh, Lonny! Lenny!" he called. "Come look at the nice little doggy!"

The girls spun around. The twins were peeking out from behind the house.

"A doggy! A doggy!" they cried.

Nancy gasped. The twins were running toward Chip and waving messy, gloppy, finger-painty hands!

6

Brenda Blabs

No!" Nancy screamed as the twins began to pet Chip. "Get back! Get back!"

Nancy watched in horror as the twins stroked Chip with their dirty hands. Soon Chip was covered with green, red, and yellow streaks.

"Quit it!" George yelled as she pulled the twins off Chip.

Nancy grabbed Orson's painting and held it over her head.

"Give it back!" Orson demanded.

"Not unless you tell me where you got that black material," Nancy said.

"Okay, okay." He sighed. "If you really want to know."

Orson picked up the black material. He shook it out. It was filled with holes.

"This used to be my magician's cape," Orson said. "When I was Orson the Awesome."

"Why did you cut it up?" Bess asked.

"I didn't think I'd need it anymore," Orson said, "now that I'm a great artist."

Nancy touched the cape. "This isn't even velvet!" she cried.

"I know," Orson said. "But it was the closest I could find. Don't tell anyone, okay?"

"Okay." Nancy sighed.

"Do you want to know another secret?" Lonny asked. He began to whisper. "Wally's not really a cockroach."

"Yeah," Lenny said. "He's a dung beetle."

"Shut up!" Orson yelled at his brothers. The twins giggled and ran away.

"Can I get back to work?" Orson asked. "I'm having my first art show tomorrow afternoon."

"Go ahead," Nancy said.

"We won't *bug* you anymore," George said.

"Cute," Orson muttered.

As the girls and Chip walked away from the Wong home, Nancy pulled out her detective notebook.

"I guess Orson is clean," Nancy said. She looked down at her paint-streaked dog. "But Chip isn't."

"And now you have only one suspect left," Bess said. "Mrs. Vanderpool."

"Should we investigate her now, Nancy?" George asked.

Nancy shook her head. "Let's do it tomorrow. I have to give Chip a bath."

Chip covered her head with her grubby paws. Then she gave a loud whine.

"Sit still, girl!" Nancy said as she tried to scrub Chip in her front yard.

Chip jumped out of the large metal basin. She was covered with soapsuds.

Nancy sighed. The red, yellow, and green paint was still stuck to her coat.

"I give up, Chip," Nancy said. "I'll have to take you to the Dashing Dog Pet Salon tomorrow. Maybe they can get out all that yucky paint."

Chip shook her wet coat. Nancy shrieked as soapy water splashed and sprayed everywhere.

But then Nancy heard someone else shriek. She looked up and saw a dripping wet Kendra Cartwright.

"Kendra!" Nancy gasped.

"Thanks a lot," Kendra sputtered. "My new blouse is sopping wet!"

"Chip didn't mean it," Nancy said.

"But *you* did," Kendra snapped.

"What do you mean?" Nancy asked.

"You ruined the black velvet coat yesterday because you wanted to wear it," Kendra said. "*All* the kids in River Heights are talking about you."

Nancy's eyes opened wide. She didn't know that the rumor had spread so quickly.

"They're wrong, Kendra," Nancy said. "I would never do anything like that."

"Yes, you would," Kendra said, sticking out her chin. "And you had help."

Kendra pulled a wet paper from under her arm. It was the latest copy of the *Carlton News*.

"Here," Kendra said. "Read this!"

Nancy looked at the paper. The gossip was on the first page. She read it out loud: "'Which soccer jock and prissy blond would do anything for their best friend? Here's a hint: They're snipping cousins!'"

Nancy felt her cheeks burn. Brenda was writing about George and Bess!

"This is another one of Brenda's rumors, Kendra!" Nancy declared. But when she looked up, Kendra was gone.

Nancy kneeled down and petted Chip's damp coat.

"Now I really have to solve this case, girl," she said, sighing. "Brenda is accusing my best friends, too!"

That night Nancy ate dinner with her father. Carson Drew was a lawyer and liked to help Nancy with her detective work.

"What if Brenda keeps writing those bad things about me, Daddy?" Nancy asked.

"Don't worry, Pudding Pie," Mr. Drew said. He sprinkled pepper on his chicken. "The truth always comes out sooner or later."

Nancy sighed. "Well, it better come *sooner*, Daddy. Because I'm being framed!"

The next morning Nancy met Bess and George. They had gotten permission to walk Chip to the Dashing Dog Pet Salon.

"She called us a soccer jock and a prissy blond," George said. She held out her own copy of the *Carlton News*. "But how do we know she meant me and Bess?"

Nancy tugged Chip's leash. "Well, you *are* a soccer jock, George. And Bess is—"

"Prissy?" Bess cried. "Is that what you think I am—prissy?"

"No!" Nancy said quickly. "You're . . . blond."

"Oh," Bess said. She twirled her ponytail. "Well, that's true."

The girls walked down Main Street. Then Nancy saw something on the sidewalk. It was a message written in colored chalk—a mean message.

"Oh, no!" Nancy cried. "It says, Nancy is a cut-up!"

Chip nuzzled Nancy's hand as her owner shook her head. "The rumor is everywhere I go. Even on Main Street."

The girls walked into the Dashing Dog. Nancy had never been inside the salon before. It had pink furniture and pictures of glamorous dogs on the walls.

"Hello. My name is Rex," a man behind a desk said. "May I help you?"

"Yes," Nancy said. "This is Chip. She's a chocolate Lab."

The man stared at the red, yellow, and green streaks on Chip's coat.

"You mean she *used* to be chocolate," he said, chuckling. "Now she's strawberry, lemon, and lime!"

The man laughed loudly at his joke. He stopped suddenly when the door opened. "Mrs. Vanderpool!" he cried. "What a pleasant surprise."

Nancy whirled around. Mrs. Vanderpool?

Mrs. Vanderpool was standing at the door with her little dogs in her arms.

The dogs were wearing little red coats—with black velvet collars!

7

Art Smart

Nancy," George whispered. "Do you see what I see?"

Nancy nodded. She looked at Mrs. Vanderpool, who was busy talking to Rex.

"It's a bit warm out there, Rex," Mrs. Vanderpool was saying.

"I guess this is what they call the dog days of August," Rex said.

"*Every* day is a dog day for me!" Mrs. Vanderpool said, hugging her Yorkies. "Quick," Nancy whispered to Bess and George. "Let's hide. I don't want Mrs. Vanderpool to see us."

Tugging Chip's leash, Nancy ducked behind a pink curtain. Bess and George followed.

"Nancy!" Bess whispered. "We're not alone. Look!"

Nancy whirled around. Sitting on high tables were dogs. One, a big poodle, had curlers in her hair; another, a bulldog, was wrapped in a fluffy towel.

"Shhh," Nancy told the dogs. She put her finger in front of her lips.

"I can't believe it," George whispered. "Mrs. Vanderpool's dogs are wearing black velvet collars!"

"I know," Nancy said. "But I don't want Mrs. Vanderpool to see us. Then she'll know we're watching her."

Nancy heard a soft growl. She looked down and saw a little Yorkie peeking underneath the curtain.

"It's Mrs. Vanderpool's dust mop," George said. "Shoo! Go away!"

The other Yorkie peeked in. They both sniffed at Chip. Then they began to bark.

"Oh, no!" Nancy said.

"What's going on back there?" Rex called from the front.

Chip barked and ducked under the curtain. Nancy, Bess, and George ran after her.

"Chip, come back!" Nancy called.

The two little Yorkies yapped as they chased Chip all around the waiting room. A woman reading a magazine screamed. A man clutched his Chihuahua to his chest.

The dogs ran across a sofa and hopped over the chairs.

"My babies!" Mrs. Vanderpool cried. "That messy dog is chasing my babies!"

"It's the other way around!" Nancy insisted as she tried to catch Chip.

The dogs kicked magazines in the air as they raced around the waiting room.

"YAP! YAP! YAP!" the Yorkies barked.

"Woof! Woof! Woof!" Chip barked back.

"Stop!" Rex shouted. "Down! Heel!"

The Yorkies jumped in front of Chip and growled. Chip began to whine. Then she ran to Nancy and leaped into her arms.

"Good girl!" Nancy said.

"Well, I never!" Mrs. Vanderpool said as she scooped up her Yorkies. "That Lab almost ruined my babies' new coats!"

Nancy handed Chip's leash to George. She walked up to Mrs. Vanderpool.

"Where did you get those black velvet collars, Mrs. Vanderpool?" Nancy asked.

"From me," Rex said. "Do you like them?"

Nancy whirled around.

"Those coats are from my brand-new doggie fashion collection," Rex said. He reached under his desk and pulled out a box. "I was going to display them today."

Nancy looked into the box. It was filled with tiny hats, sweaters, and coats. Many of them had black velvet collars.

"Rex showed them to me yesterday," Mrs. Vanderpool explained. "When I saw the coats with the black velvet collars I just had to have them!"

"But what about the black velvet coat at Peppermint Penny's?" Nancy asked.

"That was lovely," Mrs. Vanderpool said. "So I decided to order one for my granddaughter."

"Your granddaughter?" Nancy asked. She reached into her pocket and pulled out the pearl earring. "Is that why we found this in the back room yesterday?"

Mrs. Vanderpool smiled when she saw her earring.

"Yes!" Mrs. Vanderpool said. "It must have dropped off when I was checking the size of the coat. There was no one else in the stockroom at the time."

So that explains it, Nancy thought as she handed the earring back to Mrs. Vanderpool.

"Well, I just wanted to come by and show Rex how sweet my babies look," Mrs. Vanderpool said. "Bye, now!"

As Mrs. Vanderpool left the salon, her little dogs growled at Chip one last time.

"Ankle-biters!" George muttered.

"Now," Rex said, rubbing his hands. "I have the perfect denim jacket that would look fabulous on Chocolate Chip."

"No thank you," Nancy said. "She'll look fabulous right after she has a good bath."

"Oh, yes—the bath," Rex said. He took Chip's leash. "You can pick her up in about an hour."

The girls left the Dashing Dog.

"Mrs. Vanderpool was our last suspect," Bess said. "Now what are we going to do?"

"I'm not sure," Nancy said. "But I have to solve this case before Brenda writes any more nasty things about me!"

As they walked along Main Street, Nancy noticed a small crowd of people.

"What's going on?" George asked.

"It's some kind of art show," Nancy said. She looked closer. "Orson Wong's art show!"

Orson's artwork was lined up on the

sidewalk. There was a painting of an ant, a grasshopper, and of course—Wally.

"Where do you get your inspiration?" a man asked Orson.

Orson picked up Wally's glass jar. "From under a rock."

Then Nancy noticed a painting that looked different. Instead of a bug, there was some kind of brown-and-white smudge.

Bess noticed it, too. "I think someone stepped on that bug," she said.

"I don't think it's a bug, Bess," Nancy said. She got a closer look. The splotch was sprinkled with nuts and chocolate chips. "It's ice cream."

George stared at the splotch.

"It's Panda Bar ice cream!" George exclaimed. "I had a stain just like that on my soccer shirt."

"And it's not signed by Orson," Bess said. "It's signed by Lonny and Lenny."

Nancy noticed something familiar

about the black background. She reached out to touch it. It was thick and soft.

"Bess! George!" she exclaimed. "This is the velvet from the black coat!"

8

Pests Confess

Nancy felt someone grab her hand. She looked up and saw Lenny Wong.

"Hands off the merchandise, lady!" he growled.

"Yeah," Lonny said. "You break it, you buy it."

Nancy pulled her hand back. She pointed to the Panda Bar painting. "Where did that come from?" she demanded.

Lenny smiled proudly. "Orson had room in his show so we made it."

"Do you like it?" Lonny asked.

"No," Nancy snapped. "I like cherry-vanilla Panda Bars."

Lonny and Lenny looked at each other.

"Uh-oh," Lenny whispered.

"It's an ice-cream stain, isn't it?" Nancy demanded.

"No!" Lonny said quickly.

"Then what is it?" George asked.

"Um . . . it's a polar bear," Lenny said.

"In a *mudslide!*" Lonny said.

Nancy pointed to the black velvet. "Then where did you get that black velvet?" she asked.

"Is it from Peppermint Penny's cut-up coat?" Bess asked.

The twins huddled together. They looked scared.

"You don't have to answer them," a voice said.

Nancy turned around. Brenda Carlton was standing behind them.

"Everyone knows that Nancy cut up the coat," Brenda said. "It's all over town."

"Thanks to you," Bess said.

Brenda held up a small plastic change purse. "Besides, I want to buy that painting to hang over my bed."

"That's a lie!" George said. "You want to buy that painting so everyone will still think Nancy cut up the coat!"

"I don't know what you're talking about," Brenda said.

Lonny held his hand out to Brenda. "That will be fifty cents. Cough it up!"

"Nancy!" George complained. "Brenda is buying our only evidence. What are we going to do?"

"I know what to do," Bess said.

Nancy watched as Bess marched over to Orson.

"Give me that," Bess said. She grabbed the jar out of Orson's hand.

"Hey!" Orson said. "What are you doing with Wally? He's the star of the show. Like Mona Lisa."

George gasped. "Is that Bess holding that bug?"

"Bess is terrified of bugs," Nancy said.

"Hey, Brenda," Bess said as she held up the jar. "Say hello to Wally the cock-roach."

"W-W-Wally?" Brenda stammered.

Nancy and George stood behind Bess.

"Wally was in this jar all week," Bess said. She began to unscrew the lid. "I'll bet he'd love some Panda Bar ice cream."

Brenda looked at Wally. Her chin began to quiver. Then she dropped the Panda Bar painting and screamed.

"Hey, wait!" Lonny shouted as Brenda ran away. "We had a deal!"

Bess looked down at the jar. Then she screamed, too. "A cockroach! Yuck! What was I thinking?"

While Orson grabbed the jar from Bess, Nancy grabbed the twins by their shoulders.

"Tell us what happened," Nancy said. "If you don't, we'll tell Penny our-selves."

"Okay, okay," Lenny said. "Penny told

us to put our Panda Bars in the mini fridge, but we couldn't find it."

"So we put them on top of some boxes," Lonny said.

"Go on," Nancy urged.

"When everyone else was practicing on the red carpet, we went into the stockroom to eat our Panda Bars," Lenny said.

"How does that explain the coat?" George asked.

"We dripped ice cream all over the coat," Lenny said. "We didn't want Penny to find out, so we took her scissors and cut it out."

"You cut out the stain?" Nancy asked.

Lenny nodded. "And I stuffed it in my pants' pocket. That's why it looks smudgy and not drippy."

Nancy turned to Orson. "Did you know your brothers did this?"

"No way," Orson said. "I thought it was a finger painting."

The twins held up their hands and wiggled their fingers.

"We love to finger paint!" Lonny declared.

Nancy stared at the twins' hands. They were covered with colored chalk.

"You also wrote that mean message about me, didn't you?" Nancy asked.

The twins looked down at their hands.

"Busted." Lonny sighed.

"We knew you were being blamed for the coat," Lenny said. "We didn't want to get caught so we blamed you, too."

"Well, the game is over," George said. "You're going to tell Penny right now."

"But she'll never let us model clothes again!" Lonny cried.

Lenny waved his hand. "That's okay. Those sweaters were itchy."

Nancy, Bess, and George took the twins to Peppermint Penny's. The culprits stood in front of her and told her everything.

"What you did was wrong," Penny said. "But I was wrong, too. I should have had someone watch the room at all times."

After the twins apologized, they ran out of the store.

"It's too bad the coat was ruined," Bess said. "It was so pretty."

"I know," Penny said. "But you'll be seeing a lot more of that black velvet coat around River Heights."

"We will?" Nancy asked.

Penny smiled. "After the fashion show I got five orders for the coat. Without the hole, of course."

"Of course!" Nancy giggled.

As the girls left Peppermint Penny's, Nancy felt great. They had solved "The Case of the Cut-up Coat."

"Let's call Brenda and let her know, Nancy," Bess said.

Nancy thought about it. Then she shook her head. "Let's not," she said. "If a bad rumor can spread so fast, maybe a good rumor will, too."

The girls decided to celebrate at the pizza parlor. But first they went to the Dashing Dog to pick up Chip.

While Bess and George read pet magazines in the waiting room, Nancy took out her notebook. Then she began to write:

Gossip! Gossip! Gossip! It sure can hurt—especially when it's about you! I also learned something else: nice clothes are great, but being nice on the inside is so much better. And *that* never goes out of style!

Case closed.

**Do your younger brothers and sisters
want to read books like yours?**

Let them know there are books just for them!

THE
NANCY DREW
NOTEBOOKS®

Look for a brand-new story every other month

Available from Minstrel® Books
Published by Pocket Books

1356-09

The Hardy Boys® are:

THE CLUES BROTHERS™

By Franklin W. Dixon

Look for a brand-new story every other month

Sabrina
The Teenage Witch™

Salem's Tails™

What's it like to be a powerful warlock,
sentenced to one hundred years in a
cat's body for trying to take over the world?

Ask Salem.

**Read all about Salem's magical
adventures in this new series based on the
hit ABC-TV show!**

#1 CAT TV

#2 Teacher's Pet

#3 You're History

#4 The King of Cats

#5 Dog day Afternoon

Salem Goes to Rome

Now available!
Look for a new title every other month

A MINSTREL® BOOK

Published by Pocket Books

2007-03